Disney Pinocchio

This is the story of a little puppet
who follows his heart and becomes a real boy.

Once upon a time, there was a friendly cricket named Jiminy. One night, Jiminy Cricket's travels took him to the workshop of Geppetto, an old woodcarver. There were ticking clocks, musical boxes, and wonderful wooden toys everywhere.

Geppetto was putting the finishing touches on a little boy puppet.

"Now," Geppetto said, "I have just the name for you—Pinocchio!" Then he added softly, "He almost looks alive."

That evening at bedtime, Geppetto looked out of the window. Twinkling up in the sky was the Wishing Star.

"I wish I may, I wish I might, have the wish I make tonight," Geppetto said. He wished for Pinocchio to become a *real* boy.

Soon after, Geppetto, his cat Figaro, and Cleo the goldfish were fast asleep. Only Jiminy Cricket was still awake.

Suddenly, a bright blue light filled the workshop. The beautiful Blue Fairy appeared.

"Good Geppetto," she said gently. "You have given so much happiness to others. You deserve to have your wish come true."

Waving her wand over Pinocchio, she said:
"*Little puppet made of pine,*
Wake! The gift of life is thine."

Magically, Pinocchio began to stir.
"I can move!" he said in amazement. "I can talk!"
"Prove yourself brave, truthful, and unselfish," said the
Blue Fairy, "and some day you will be a *real* boy."
The Fairy asked Jiminy Cricket to be Pinocchio's
conscience, to teach him right from wrong. "Now remember,
Pinocchio," she added, "be a good boy and always let your
conscience be your guide." And with that she disappeared.

Geppetto woke up and saw Pinocchio walking and talking! At first he thought he must be dreaming, but then he realized his wish had come true. Geppetto was so happy, he began to play a merry tune for everyone to dance to.

Next morning, Geppetto sent Pinocchio off to school. On the way, two villains, a fox called Honest John and his friend, a cat called Gideon, spotted Pinocchio skipping happily along.

Honest John cried, "A live puppet without strings!" He could sell him to Stromboli's Puppet Show and make *lots* of money!

The villains convinced the little puppet that becoming an actor would be much more fun than school! Jiminy tried to stop Pinocchio from leaving with the villains, but Pinocchio was too excited to listen.

That night, Pinocchio sang and danced merrily in the puppet show. The audience clapped and cheered with delight. Pinocchio was a star!

However, when the little puppet asked to go home, Stromboli, the owner of the show, roared with anger. He locked Pinocchio in a cage and bellowed, "This will be your home now!"

Alone and frightened, Pinocchio sobbed, "I should have listened to you, Jiminy."

Suddenly, the Blue Fairy appeared and said: "Pinocchio, why didn't you go to school?" The little puppet was afraid to tell the truth. "Two big monsters with big green eyes…" he fibbed. "Well, I… they tied me in a big sack…"

As soon as Pinocchio told this lie, his nose began to grow! The more Pinocchio lied, the longer his nose grew!

"Perhaps you haven't been telling the truth, Pinocchio," said the Blue Fairy. "A lie keeps growing and growing until it's as plain as the nose on your face."

"I'll never lie again!" promised the little puppet.

So the Blue Fairy gently touched Pinocchio's nose with her wand and turned it back to normal. She unlocked the cage and set him free.

"Come on, Pinoke!" cried Jiminy. But as the little puppet raced after Jiminy, he met up with...

...Honest John and Gideon again. This time, they persuaded Pinocchio that he was ill and needed a holiday at a wonderful place called Pleasure Island.

The two villains sold Pinocchio to a wicked coachman, who put him on a coach full of very noisy, naughty boys.

Luckily, Jiminy was able to climb onto the coach just as it drove off.

Pleasure Island was like a giant fun fair. The boys could have anything they wanted and be as naughty as they liked.

Jiminy thought there was something strange about Pleasure Island and begged Pinocchio to leave. But the little puppet refused to listen to Jiminy. He wanted to stay and play pool with his new friend, Lampwick.

Finally, Jiminy gave up and decided to go home on his own.

Just as Jiminy was leaving, he saw the wicked coachman loading crates of donkeys onto a boat. One of the donkeys was crying and begging to go home to his mother.

Jiminy was shocked! Somehow, all the boys on Pleasure Island were being turned into donkeys! Jiminy raced off to rescue Pinocchio.

But by the time Jiminy found his friend, Pinocchio had already grown long, hairy ears and a tail!

"Come on! Quick!" cried Jiminy. "This way, Pinoke!"

Jiminy and Pinocchio escaped from the island by jumping into the sea and swimming home.

Cold and tired, they finally reached Geppetto's house—only to find out that Geppetto had gone looking for Pinocchio across the sea and had been swallowed by a big whale named Monstro!

Pinocchio was determined to find his father no matter how dangerous it would be. He and Jiminy headed back into the sea.

Pinocchio and Jiminy asked the fish and sea horses for help. But as soon as they heard Monstro's name, the sea creatures sped off in terror.

Meanwhile, not too far away, Monstro was waking up from a long sleep. The whale was so hungry that he gulped down a large school of fish. Without realizing, he managed to swallow Pinocchio, too!

Deep inside the whale's tummy, Pinocchio and his father were overjoyed to see each other again.

Pinocchio thought of a plan to escape. They'd build a fire to make lots of smoke inside Monstro.

"We'll make him sneeze!" said Pinocchio excitedly.

Pinocchio's plan worked! As clouds of black smoke filled Monstro's tummy, he gave an *enormous* sneeze—and out they all came on a little raft!

But as the whale crashed through the water, the little raft toppled over. Everyone was thrown into the sea and Geppetto couldn't swim! Pinocchio kept his father afloat and dragged him to the shore.

Minutes later, Jiminy found
Geppetto, Figaro, and Cleo safely
on the beach. But the little puppet
was lying face down in the water.
He wasn't moving. Heartbroken,
Geppetto took his son home.

Geppetto knelt over Pinocchio and wept. Just then, the Blue Fairy's dazzling light filled the room once again. "Prove yourself brave, truthful, and unselfish, and some day you will be a *real* boy," said the Fairy gently. "Awake, Pinocchio, awake."

Immediately, a bright light surrounded Pinocchio and he woke up! He was no longer made of wood—he was a real boy at last!

"Father, I'm alive! See?" Pinocchio cried out in delight.

"This calls for a celebration!" Geppetto cried joyfully. Jiminy proudly watched Pinocchio playing happily with his father. Now he knew that if you wish upon a star, your dreams really can come true!